our
generation

This is Coral's story.

C O R A L ™

STUCK IN THE MIDDLE OF KNOWHERE

BY

SUSAN CAPPADONIA LOVE

ILLUSTRATED BY TRISH ROUELLE

An Our Generation® *book*

MAISON BATTAT INC. *Publisher*

A very special thanks to the editor, Joanne Burke Casey.

Our Generation® Books is a registered trademark of Maison Battat Inc.
Text copyright © 2017 by Susan Love

ISBN: 978-0-9794542-6-4
Printed in China

This book is dedicated to
curious, funny, wonderful you!

Read all the adventures in the
Our Generation® Book Series

One Smart Cookie
featuring Hally™

Blizzard on Moose Mountain
featuring Katelyn™

Stars in Your Eyes
featuring Sydney Lee™

The Note in the Piano
featuring Mary Lyn™

*The Mystery of the
Vanishing Coin*
featuring Eva®

Adventures at Shelby Stables
featuring Lily Anna®

The Sweet Shoppe Mystery
featuring Jenny™

The Jumpstart Squad
featuring Juliet™

The Dress in the Window
featuring Audrey-Ann®

The Jukebox Babysitters
featuring Ashley-Rose®

In the Limelight
featuring Evelyn®

*The Most Fantabulous
Pajama Party Ever*
featuring Willow™

Magic Under the Stars
featuring Shannon™

*The Circus and the
Secret Code*
featuring Alice™

A Song from My Heart
featuring Layla™

Home Away from Home
featuring Ginger™

The Curious Castle
featuring Reese™

*Stuck in the Middle
of Knowhere*
featuring Coral™

Read more about **Our Generation®** books and dolls online:
www.ogdolls.com

CONTENTS

Chapter One	Not What I Expected	Page 9
Chapter Two	Fiona's Riddles	Page 19
Chapter Three	Why Me	Page 26
Chapter Four	Bad Surf Day	Page 34
Chapter Five	A New Friend	Page 41
Chapter Six	The Triple Dip	Page 47
Chapter Seven	Big and Crabby	Page 57
Chapter Eight	A Business Is Born	Page 64
Chapter Nine	Flibberbumbles	Page 72
Chapter Ten	Facing My Fears	Page 78
Chapter Eleven	Glad to Be Glamping	Page 90
Chapter Twelve	Use Your Head	Page 97

EXTRA! EXTRA! READ ALL ABOUT IT!
Big words, wacky words, powerful words, funny words…
what do they all mean? They are marked with this symbol *.
Look them up in the Glossary at the end of this book.

Chapter One

NOT WHAT I EXPECTED

"Waaaaa-hooooo!" I yelled into the wind. There I was, riding along with my dad in his white, open-top SUV*, the fresh breeze blowing my hair in all directions.

Beach house here I come! I thought.

I had just arrived on the tropical* island to live with my dad, my new stepmom, Iris, and my eleven-year-old stepsister, Fiona, for the summer.

Being with Fiona would be like having an instant best friend. We'd be together every day, surfing, paddleboarding and hanging out at the beach.

What a life!

I'm a city girl, and I love everything about the city. The apartment where my mom and I live on the ninth floor. The busy streets. The buses whooshing by. The lights which make the city look like it's awake all night.

But I was beyond excited to spend three months in a place known for its amazing waves and miles and miles of sandy beaches.

Me, a surfer girl! And best yet, my dad told me we would be living in a beach house.

Never mind that my stomach still felt topsy-turvy* from the ferryboat ride to the island. It was going to be a spectacular summer.

We turned onto a dirt road and a cloud of dust trailed behind us. Our SUV rolled to a stop.

"Here we are!" Pop said.

I eagerly hopped out and looked around.

As far as I could tell, we were in a jungle at the end of a dirt trail.

"I don't see it, Pop," I replied. "Where's our beach house?"

"It's straight ahead, Coral," my dad called out, his voice muffled*. He was leaning into the back of the SUV, wrestling with my suitcase to get it unstuck from between the seats.

I stared straight ahead. Nothing but trees. Then I checked out the area to my left and right. More nothing but trees. I didn't see the beach house. In fact, I didn't see a house at all, *or* the beach.

Hmmmm, I thought. *Strange.*

My dad laughed. "Straight ahead and *up.*"

I followed the direction of his finger and my eyes traveled up an enormous tree trunk. I gasped. Tucked into the branches of the tree was a small house!

"We're living in a *tree?*" I asked.

Pop laughed again. "Remember I told you we live in a tree house?"

"Oh, I thought you said *beach* house," I whined*.

Birds and monkeys and squirrels are meant to live in trees, I thought. *But people? People are not meant to live in trees. Play in trees, but not live in them.*

Maybe he sensed my disappointment. "Well, I guess you could say it's a beach house, too. I

mean, we are by the beach. Come and look."

We headed down a very short path made of wooden planks. The path was lined with palm trees and led to a white, sandy beach that looked like something on a postcard. Half of a huge orange sun seemed to be dipping behind the bright, blue ocean.

I wiggled my toes into the cool sand. In front of me was the surf*. Behind me I could see our tree house poking up out of the leaves.

"Pop," I asked, "how do you get up to the tree house? Will you, Iris, Fiona and I all fit in there? Why does—"

"That's the 'curious Coral' I know and love," he teased, using the nickname he gave me years ago. "Always asking how things work, why this and why that."

"You forgot to say that I drive everyone bananas with all my questions," I reminded him.

Pop grinned. "That, too." He put his arm around my shoulder. "C'mon, let me give you the grand tour of our home."

13

A couple of minutes later, my dad and I were climbing a very tall spiral staircase that went up and around and up and around (76 steps high!). It brought us to the front door of the tree house, which is actually in the back. That's why I couldn't see it at first. It was hidden by leaves.

Hanging by the door was a sign that read:

Home
♥ tweet ♥
home

Pop swung the door open for me. "C'mon in."

The first thing I noticed was the wonderful smell.

"Mmmm, yum!" I said.

"Are you baking your famous macaroni and cheese casserole?"

"I sure am," my dad told me. "I know how much you like it."

The tree house was cozy inside and decorated

like a real house. There was a couch, a coffee table with a checkers game on it, pictures on the walls and bookshelves.

"Check this out," my dad told me. "It's a lookout tower, too."

We went out on the porch, which wrapped around two sides of the tree house. Whoa! The view from up high was incredible!

It wasn't that dark yet, so I could see a few small shops in the center of the village. Pop pointed out the beach where he runs the Surf Shack.

The Surf Shack is a cabin with a thatched* roof where people can buy or rent surfboards, paddleboards and bicycles, or get them repaired.

"And right there," he said, pointing to a dock, "is where you came in on the Triple Dip." That's the name of the ferryboat that Iris runs back and forth to the mainland*, where I live with my mom.

"There it is now," he added, "bringing in the last load of passengers today."

I spotted the Triple Dip puttering toward the

dock. My dad explained that some of the people on the boat are tourists and some are people who live on the island but work on the mainland.

My dad pointed a large flashlight in the direction of the dock and clicked the on/off button several times.

"Why did you do that?" I asked.

"If I flash the light three times, it lets Iris and Fiona know that dinner is almost ready," he said. "Two times means we're having a beach cookout."

"Can I try it?" I asked. "Just in case they didn't see it the first time?"

"Sure," my dad replied.

Maybe living in a tree house will be fun after all, I decided.

"Most people send a text message or call each other on their phones," I said. "But not us, because we have a secret flashlight code."

"But no phone," Pop added.

"You mean you don't have a phone?" I asked.

"Not here," he replied. "There's one at the

Surf Shack. That's the phone that I use when we talk, and you can use it to call your mom every day."

He continued, "There's also no TV, no electricity, no way to get onto the Internet, no—"

No just about everything that I am used to! I thought glumly*. *What have I gotten myself into?*

Chapter Two

FIONA'S RIDDLES

It would be just like my dad to be kidding around about having no electricity. He's always teasing me.

But I soon realized he wasn't joking. There was no computer in sight. No dishwasher or microwave or toaster or oven, either. So where was that macaroni and cheese casserole smell coming from?

I noticed an old, light blue blender on the dining table. It was filled with a bunch of pink and yellow flowers. I supposed that was a good use for the blender since there was no electricity.

"Hmmmm...where are the beds?" I asked my dad, almost afraid to hear the answer. I imagined my dad, Iris, Fiona and me perching in a tree like owls.

"Hammocks," my dad explained. "You'll be surprised how comfy they are."

A tree house instead of a beach house. Flashlights instead of phones. Hammocks instead of beds. *What's next?* I thought.

A few minutes later, when my stepmom and stepsister came home, my dad asked Fiona and me to get the macaroni and cheese out of the oven on the porch.

"Sure, Dad," Fiona agreed happily.

It felt a little strange to hear someone else calling my dad *her* dad.

Fiona slipped padded oven mitts onto her hands. She lifted the glass top from a box with shiny metal pieces on all four sides that stuck up in the air and looked like mirrors. Fiona carefully took the casserole out of the box.

I noticed the box did not have a plug and it wasn't connected to anything. "That's an oven?" I asked.

"Yep," Fiona replied. "It's our sun oven. See these mirrored flaps? They direct the sun into the box to cook the food inside."

Iris rubbed her hand in a circle on her stomach. "Yum! It looks and smells scrumptious."

"Wait until you try Fiona's sunbaked apple pie," Pop told me, as we all gobbled up our meal. "It's delish!"

After dinner, we played a game of checkers under the light of the solar lantern. I was the champ! Then Fiona showed me how to set up our "beds."

Metal rings on the ends of the colorfully striped hammocks were hung on hooks attached to the tree house walls. The hammocks stretched from one wall to the opposite wall. Fiona's hammock and my hammock both had a view through the window of the starry sky and ocean.

My hammock swung lightly as I snuggled under a cozy throw* in the hammock with my fluffy, stuffed pink kitty.

As we settled down to sleep, Fiona whispered, "Coral, repeat after me. Star light, star bright, first star I see tonight. Wish I may, wish I might, get the wish I wish tonight."

I repeated the rhyme and wished for the best summer vacation ever. But long after everyone else had fallen asleep, I was still wide-awake.

It was too quiet! I was used to drifting off to sleep while listening to the sounds of the city: the

22

hum of traffic, cars beeping and trucks clunking down the road. The only noise on the island was from the waves softly tumbling onto the shore.

And it was too dark. There were no bright streetlights peeking in through my bedroom window. The only lights were from the stars.

So many thoughts were racing around in my brain. I was missing my mom. Since my parents divorced, I had always spent summers with my dad. But I was still close-by my mom because Pop had lived in the city, too.

Then a few months ago, when he and Iris got married, he moved to the island. He was excited about running the Surf Shack because, back in the day*, he was a top surfer.

My dad had promised that he'd give me surfing lessons when business was slow at the Surf Shack.

Then I'll be a real surfer girl, I thought. I couldn't wait! The city where I live on the mainland is a long drive from the ocean. Before my boat ride to the island that day, I'd never been to the ocean.

To make life even sweeter, I'd be on the island when the Surfing and Sand Sculpture* Competition* took place at the end of the month. How great was that?

Another thing I was looking forward to was getting to know Fiona better during the next couple of months.

I remembered the only other time I had met Fiona. It was at our parents' wedding celebration, which took place on the roof deck of the 26th floor of a hotel in the city. Fiona and I hadn't talked much, though, because she wasn't feeling well.

I'd expected to spend the summer with the quiet Fiona I'd met at the wedding. But the Fiona I'd met on the ferryboat when coming to the island earlier that day was bubbly and confident and a completely different person.

Before the boat left the dock, just as I was waving goodbye to my mom, Fiona had called out, "All aboard the Triple Dip! Last call for the boat to nowhere!"

I thought I hadn't heard Fiona right. "Where

did you say we're going?" I asked her.

"Nowhere," Fiona replied. "That's where home tweet home is."

Nowhere? Home tweet home? At the time, that made no sense.

Then, during the boat ride, Fiona told me. "I was surprised that you agreed to come glamping with us this summer."

Glamping? What was that supposed to mean?

Why is my stepsister always talking in riddles? I wondered, as I finally dozed off to sleep.

Chapter Three

WHY ME

"Let's take the tunnel instead of the stairs," Fiona suggested early the next morning. "It's quicker."

I thought Fiona was talking in riddles again. She pointed to a green door covered with signs that read:

Fiona slid the green door to the left. In front of us was a huge curving green tube that looked like it belonged on a playground. It was a giant slide!

Quick as a wink, Fiona slid down feet first. Then *whoosh!* I went, too—whooping with delight until my feet hit the ground. Next, out popped Iris, followed by my dad.

Iris and Fiona set off for the ferry while my dad and I headed down the beach to the Surf Shack.

Pop was wearing a red T-shirt and a nametag that read:

> **Welcome to the Surf Shack! My name is**
> # Bigboss

When we got to the shop, the first thing I did was call my mom. I filled her in about the tree house, the sun oven and the slide.

"Wow!" my mom exclaimed. "It's going to

be quite a summer!"

"Definitely interesting," I replied.

"What else is going on there?" she asked.

"Fiona said the Triple Dip is getting really busy," I told my mom. "Lots of people are coming to the island for the Surfing and Sand Sculpture Competition. It will take place right in front of the Surf Shack."

"That sounds really fun," my mom said. "How was the ferryboat ride?"

"Well, I felt queasy* from the waves," I told her. "Did you know they use the boat to take people out snorkeling*, too?"

"Oh, I hope you get to do that while you're there," said my mom.

"I'm not sure if I will or not. The snorkeling tours are completely sold out until the end of the summer," I told her. "They're very popular."

We talked until it was time for my mom to leave for work. After we hung up, I felt homesick and a little sad.

My dad was helping a customer. I wanted

to "do" something, not just stand around. I introduced myself to a guy who works at the shop. He sort of half waved, without a hello.

"Hi there! I'm Coral!" I stuck out my hand to shake his but he had already turned his back to me. He was fixing the tire on a green bicycle.

Every once in a while I heard him mutter* things like, "Crud-macker!" and "Awwwwwsugar snap peas!" and "Dibberdabber-wallensnaff!"

I hadn't caught his name, but I was pretty sure it wasn't Mr. Happy.

I circled around the bike he was working on and took a peek at his nametag.

Welcome to the Surf Shack! My name is

Grump

I couldn't help asking, "Is your name really Grump?"

"Stick around for a while, Coral," my dad joked, "and you'll understand—"

Suddenly, a huge CRASH! interrupted my dad. Grump's tools were spilled all over the floor. "Oh, coconuts!" Grump huffed. "Swizzle-swazzle bing-bang!"

My dad flashed me a smile and a wink that said, "See what I mean?"

After I helped Grump put all the tools back in the toolbox, there really was nothing for me to do at the Surf Shack. My dad was at the beach giving paddleboarding lessons to a couple who were on their honeymoon*.

I read the papers and posters tacked on the Shack's corkboard: "Free Purple Couch!"; "Need a Friendly and Fun Dog Walker and Cat Sitter?"; "Beach Concert Every Tuesday Night."

I drank some water, twirled my hair around my finger and whistled a made-up song. I re-laced my orange and pink sneakers and counted backward from 100. I thought about how bored I was.

I hopped on one foot over to Grump. "Why

30

is there no electricity on the island?" I asked.

"There is," he told me. "The shops and hotels in the village use wind-powered electricity."

"But why?" I continued.

Grump sighed. "Because a lot of folks here try to preserve* the beauty of the island," he explained. "There's no reason to use up all our natural resources* if we don't have to."

"Don't you miss having a computer?" I asked Grump.

"Not really." Grump rolled his eyes. "I'd rather read and play beach volleyball and surf."

"Speaking of surfing, why are surfboards so long?" I asked.

"Why, why, why," Grump grumbled under his breath. He closed his eyes, shaking his head slowly.

"Why is the ocean so blue here?" I asked him. "Why is the sand so white?"

Grump got up and went to the counter under the cash register, opened the drawer, and pulled out a blank nametag. He wrote on the front of it with a blue marker and then handed it to me.

Well, isn't that just the nicest thing to do? I thought. *My own Surf Shack nametag!* I glanced* at it:

> **Welcome to the Surf Shack! My name is**
> # Why

"Why did you write 'Why' on my nametag?" I asked in a disappointed tone as I pinned it onto my shirt.

"Exactly!" Grump snorted, as if I'd just said something funny. "Because you ask a lot of questions. And I'm in charge of making the nametags."

Chapter Four

BAD SURF DAY

The next two days seemed like they lasted two years. They dragged on and on.

Thanks to the upcoming Surfing and Sand Sculpture Competition, customers came to the Surf Shack nonstop.

One of the Shack's surfing instructors was on vacation, so that meant my dad was especially busy, either running the cash register or giving surfing and paddleboarding lessons.

Good for business, but not so good for me. It seemed like I was in the way at the shop. I had no real "job." I'd already finished reading three of the four books I'd brought to the island.

Pop hadn't had time yet to give me my first surfing lesson. There was no one to go swimming with, either.

Where was Fiona, the instant best friend I thought I'd have on the island? She was on the ferryboat with Iris.

Fiona had told me that she would *live* on the boat if she could. That's how much she loves it.

I bet I'm the only girl with a stepsister who lives in a tree but wishes she could live on the ocean, I thought.

My fourth day on the island was the worst yet. A disaster* actually.

Pop had promised that after the Surf Shack closed that day he would give me my first surfing lesson.

Grump gives a water safety lesson to everyone who rents gear at the Surf Shack, so I listened in while he was with a group that was renting surfboards.

He started out with the basics, like the importance of sunscreen and not leaving anything behind on the beach such as water bottles or trash.

Then he talked for a while about ocean safety, including wearing a wetsuit or rash guard for protection if you fall, or from the sun, or from very cold water.

Grump also explained surfing etiquette, which is a big word for manners.

"Share the water and be polite. When you're riding your bike on a bicycle path or sidewalk," Grump told the group, "you try to stay out of the way of other people. You do the same thing on waves by not getting in the path of other surfers."

Grump's last word of advice was to always use the buddy system. That means going out with another person who's an adult. It's dangerous to swim or surf alone.

All day long I could hardly wait until Pop and I grabbed surfboards and got into the water.

I had learned to swim in a pool. I'd never been swimming in a pond or lake, much less an ocean, so I was counting the minutes until the Shack closed.

I imagined myself riding a big wave. A really really really enormous wave.

Finally it was closing time. I put on a pink and yellow wetsuit, which Fiona had lent to me for the summer.

Pop let me pick out my very own surfboard. I chose a light green one with a white wave design at the top.

First we placed my surfboard on the dry sand to practice.

Next we did some stretching exercises to warm up our muscles. Pop showed me how to attach the leash.

"Even if you fall," Pop told me, "the surfboard can't float away because the leash goes around your ankle and connects to the board."

My dad showed me how to get out in the water by lying on my stomach on the surfboard and using my arms to paddle to a wave. He also explained how to push up from paddling to standing in one motion, which is called a pop up.

That seemed pretty easy. *This is going to be a piece of cake*,* I thought. *No problem!*

We headed into the water. I was grinning as

big as the ocean is wide.

My grin turned into a feeling of horror as a stringy and slimy something slid across my right ankle. Eww!

"Help!" I hollered. "Pop!"

The more I tried to shake the sea creature off of me, the more it tangled around my leg.

I grabbed my ankle and screamed. A wave crashed into me and knocked me over, and then my legs flipped up into the air.

I accidentally snorted water into my nose. Just before my head was dunked underwater by the next wave, I realized the sea creature was actually just a small piece of seaweed.

My dad came hopping over the waves with his surfboard tucked under his arm. "I'm coming!" he yelled.

Another wave washed over me. "I'm drowning!" I sputtered.

"You can stand up here, honey," Pop said in a soothing voice. He bent down and reached for my arm. I noticed that the water was a little above his knees.

The water is less than three feet deep? I thought, feeling silly. I scrambled up, choking and coughing.

Just as I calmed myself down, something nibbled at my big toe on my left foot! "Crab attack!" I shrieked. "Giant child-eating crab!"

Pop dipped his hand into the sand and pulled up an empty seashell. He patted my back. "It can be scary at first, Coral. Are you OK?"

"I'm not OK!" I cried, leaping over the waves all the way to the shore. "And I am never ever *ever* going in the ocean *again*."

Chapter Five

A NEW FRIEND

I put the surfboard back against the shack wall and went inside to change out of my wetsuit. Once I'd cooled down, I apologized to my dad for getting so upset.

Pop asked me if I'd like to try again the next day. I shook my head, sure that there was no way I'd get up enough nerve to go back in the ocean.

Surfing was out of the question. *It's like I'm stranded on an island in the middle of nowhere with nothing to do!* I thought.

A singsong voice interrupted my not-so-great mood.

"Sweet, juicy pineapple!" a woman called out. She was rolling a boxy cart on big rubber wheels along the beach. "Sliced fresh!"

As she got closer, I noticed that the woman

was wearing a silver crown sparkling with red, blue and green crystals.

Sweet, fresh pineapple sounded so yummy that it made me forget all about the surfing disaster. Pop gave me some money and I skipped down the beach to catch up with the woman.

"Jane Dilly at your service," she told me. In about ten seconds she peeled the pineapple, cut it into chunks and split them into three cups: one for Pop, one for Grump and one for me.

When I held out two dollars to pay for the fruit, Jane Dilly put her hand up like a stop sign and smiled. "This one's on me. Just my way of saying that I'm glad you're joining us on the island this summer."

"Thank you," I said.

Jane Dilly smiled and waved goodbye. "See you tomorrow, honey. Same time, same place."

The pineapple was sweet and juicy. It was love at first bite! I closed my eyes and enjoyed every taste.

"Hey!" someone said. "Aren't you Fiona's

new sister?"

My eyes flew open. A boy was standing in front of me. "Stepsister," I corrected him. "And yes, I am."

"I thought so," he stated. "I'm Josh. I see that you already met the Pineapple Princess. She's my mom." He pointed to Jane Dilly, who was cutting a pineapple for a customer.

So that explains the crown, I thought.

Josh looked about my age, maybe a little younger. He was wearing a T-shirt that read:

Welcome
to Knowhere

"There's a spelling mistake on your T-shirt," I told Josh. "The word 'nowhere' doesn't start with a K." As the words were coming out of my mouth, I remembered what Fiona had said on the Triple Dip about the boat to nowhere.

Josh looked down at his shirt. "It's spelled right."

"Nope, it's not," I replied.

Josh looked confused. Then his lips curled up into a smile. "Um, you know that this is Knowhere, right?"

"You better believe it," I said. "No electricity, no way to get onto the Internet, and wild animals as our only neighbors…this is definitely nowhere."

Josh thought that was hilarious*. He laughed so hard that he fell over and flopped onto the sand,

holding his stomach.

What's up with this boy? I thought as I stared down at him.

"Why," he said, calling me by the name on my nametag. "Knowhere is the place you're standing this very minute."

"I got that!" I snapped. "And my name is not Why!"

"I mean," he replied, "Knowhere, with a K, is the name of this island!"

Oh, gee! I smacked the side of my head lightly. How had I never asked the name of the island? That's so not like me. Asking questions is what I do. I'd always just called it "The Island" or "Pop's Island."

"There's a pretty good story behind the name of this island," Josh explained. "A few hundred years ago, three explorers discovered the island. They thought it was so beautiful that they didn't want other people to know about it.

"The explorers wanted to keep the island for themselves so they made a promise: it would be their secret island. No one else would *know where* it was. And that's how they named the island 'Knowhere.'"

   Perfect, I thought. *I really am stuck in the middle of Knowhere.*

Chapter Six

THE TRIPLE DIP

Thanks to Grump, hardly anybody called me Coral anymore. Even Fiona called me Why, when I saw her that is, which wasn't that much.

At night, Fiona and I would play games, bake potatoes wrapped in foil on the beach fire, and watch for shooting stars outside the tree house window. But during the day, she always tagged along with Iris on the ferryboat.

The island is beautiful, but it's nothing like the city, so it did not feel like home to me yet.

Life in the city was busy busy busy all the time, filled with theater and art classes, softball practice and violin lessons. It was much more relaxed on the island.

A bright spot in my day was when Josh and his mom rolled by with their fruit cart. Pop,

Grump and I always split a pineapple.

While Jane Dilly cut it into cubes, Josh and I would goof around or play a fun game called "Mancala." We dug 14 small holes in the wet sand to create the playing "board" and used smooth pebbles from the beach as playing pieces.

The goal is to take turns and move the pebbles around the board to collect as many pebbles as possible before the game ends. (The directions are at the end of this book.)

While we were playing, I mentioned to Josh that I was afraid of going back in the ocean and swimming with living creatures. "Especially sharks," I told him.

"Sharks?!" he hooted. "Bah! They're *Knowhere* to be found. Get it? Knowhere? Like nowhere…"

"I get it," I groaned. "Bad joke."

"Made you laugh," he said, grinning.

From then on, he sprinkled "Knowhere jokes" into our conversation.

For example, when he saw me sitting in the

Surf Shack wearing my wetsuit, snorkeling mask and fins, Josh remarked, "Looks like you're all dressed up with *Knowhere* to go."

Once, when Josh's bike got a flat tire, he asked, "*Knowhere* I can find Grump?"

As silly as the jokes were, they always made me smile.

The Triple Dip delivered supplies from the mainland to businesses on the beach twice a week. One Wednesday morning, we heard the boat's anchor go "kerplunk!" into the water in front of the Surf Shack. Pop waved and jogged over to it.

I raced along behind, eager to help him, Iris and Fiona unload boxes and bags from the boat. *I hope they remembered to buy a candy bar for me like I asked,* I thought.

As the boat bobbed in the water, I got a good look at the writing on its side.

The Triple Dip

Fiona was standing on the bow* of the boat. "Hi, Why! I have two surprises for you. Which do you want first? Surprise number one?" Fiona asked, as she wiggled her right hand behind her back and crinkled what sounded like a candy wrapper.

"Or surprise number two?" she said, holding up two fingers on her left hand.

"Surprise number one!" I shouted.

"Ta-da!" Fiona held out a Choco-Champ, my very favorite candy bar. Nuts, crisps and gooey caramel are covered with melt-in-your-mouth dark chocolate.

"Thank you thank you thank you!" I exclaimed, reaching for it. "Do you want a bite?"

"Sure. But aren't you curious about surprise number two?" Fiona asked. "It's even better than surprise number one."

"*Another* Choco-Champ!?" I asked happily.

Fiona laughed. "No, you goofball. Someone had to cancel their reservations to go snorkeling today. So there's room on the boat. Do you want to come?"

"What a surprise that is," I said, pretending to be excited. Inside my head I was thinking about the surfing disaster when the slimy seaweed wouldn't let go of my leg and I thought a crab was tasting my foot.

Fiona clapped her hands. "So you'll come?"

"You know," I replied slowly, trying to think up an excuse. "You know...I mean, I really think that I'd better stay here to help. It's going to be a busy afternoon at the Shack."

"Could you give Coral this afternoon off?" Iris asked my dad.

"Of course," my dad agreed. "You'll love snorkeling, Coral. It's amazing to see the fish right up close."

That did it. There was no way I was going to get in the water with the fish. "Maybe after the competition is over. I just wouldn't feel right leaving you and Grump."

Pop glanced at Iris and they both shrugged*. Fiona looked disappointed.

"It's slow at the Shack right now," I said to Fiona. "Maybe I could help make deliveries in the boat with you for a while." Being in the boat seemed safer than being in the water, even if it meant I might feel seasick.

The Triple Dip

"Sure!" Iris said. "Hop in!"

As we cruised around the island, I asked Iris and Fiona about the ferryboat. "Why is it called The Triple Dip?"

Fiona looked proud. "Triple means three. And we're three businesses in one. We're a water taxi. We do snorkeling tours. And we buy supplies and groceries on the mainland and deliver them to people here."

"I like that name," I said. "Why are there big black tiles on top of this boat?"

"Those are solar panels. They soak up the sun and create electricity that powers the boat's motor," Iris explained.

"As you know, people on this island try to protect nature," Fiona added. "Unlike boats that run on gasoline and pollute the water, ours runs on sunshine, and that's one thing we'll never run out of!"

At the first stop on the beach, we saw a huge dragon wearing slippers—made completely of sand!

At the next stops, there were even more things made out of sand. A snowman, mother and baby penguins, a hand with two fingers pointing up and making a peace sign, and a winking man in the moon.

I was amazed. "Sometimes when I tried to make sand castles in a sandbox at the playground they fell apart. Why doesn't the sand on these crumble?" I asked. "Do they use glue?"

"Just sand and water," Iris said. "But the artists pack the sand together tightly."

"But why would people waste time doing something that is going to get washed away by the waves or ruined by the wind and rain?" I wondered.

"The artists are practicing for the sand sculpture competition," Fiona reminded me.

Late that night at the tree house, Fiona told me one of the reasons she'd been spending so much time on the ferryboat.

Some of the best surfers in the world were arriving on the island for the competition. Fiona wanted to be on the boat to meet them.

"This is my autograph book," she told me.

"What's an autograph?" I asked as I flipped through the small book. Some of the pages were blank, but others had handwriting on them.

"See? All these surfers signed their names in my book," she told me.

I saw that Fiona had also taped photos in the book of surfers riding waves.

Here I was, too afraid to go in the water up to my waist, and these daring surfers were out there on huge curling waves. They were doing incredible maneuvers* and tricks, some of them in the air.

"OK, time to go to bed," my dad said.

"You mean go to hammock," I replied, which made Fiona giggle.

I could hardly keep my eyes open as we snuggled into our hammocks.

Fiona whispered to me, "I'm glad we're a

blended family, Why."

There she goes talking in riddles again, I thought, but was too tired to ask: *A blender family? What is that?*

I guessed that it must have something to do with that old, blue blender that we were using as a vase.

Chapter Seven

BIG AND CRABBY

Time flew by, and soon I was getting used to life in the tree house. Sometimes, though, I just wished I could play a game on the computer or watch TV.

There was no dishwasher. Fiona and I *were* the dishwashers! And no DVD player or alarm clock, either.

"Who needs an alarm clock when we have the birds?" my dad teased.

"That's why we call this home tweet home," Iris added.

They were talking about the birds dressed in bright yellow, blue and red feathers that perched right outside our windows. As soon as the sun rose, they all began chirping and singing at once.

It's funny how in the city I lived up high in

an apartment and on the island I lived up high in a tree.

Both have beautiful but different views. One looks out onto skyscrapers, airplanes and busy streets and the other looks out at the trees, ocean and beach.

I snapped my fingers. "Bingo!" I exclaimed.

"Huh?" Fiona asked sleepily. We were washing our breakfast dishes, but Fiona was still waking up.

"I just figured out what I'm going to make for the sand sculpture contest," I told her.

"You're going to enter the contest?" Fiona asked in a surprised voice. "I thought you said making sand sculptures is a waste of time."

"Well, I changed my mind," I admitted. "And I have a great idea."

"Which is...?" Fiona asked.

"I'm going to build a model* of my whole city out of sand," I said. "With people and cars and buildings and—"

"That sounds really big," Fiona told me.

"Maybe you should start practicing by making something smaller."

That made sense. But what? I put my hands on my hips and tapped my left foot impatiently*.

Aha! My left foot reminded me of the so-called crab attack, which gave me a picture in my imagination of what my sculpture could be.

"Stop by the Surf Shack later to see my surprise sand sculpture," I told Fiona.

All the way to the Surf Shack I thought about what I could use for tools. I borrowed a plastic cup and spoon from Grump. After he heard that I was planning on entering the contest, a big bucket appeared beside me when I wasn't looking.

I found large, white half shells on the beach that were perfect for digging, plus sticks for making small details.

Every person that stopped by the Shack made comments about the sand sculpture, like, "You should move the crab's claw forward a bit"

or "Put that crab on a surfboard" or "Wouldn't it be adorable if the crab was wearing a clown hat?"

It seemed that everyone had an opinion except Josh. The minute he saw what I was doing, he jumped right in to help me, dunking the bucket into the waves to fill it and keep the sand wet.

Josh didn't give advice, or make suggestions, or tell me what I was doing wrong. He just worked beside me.

As I made tweaks* to the crab, people's comments were changing to, "That rocks, Why!" and "That's the sweetest crab I've ever seen!"

By noontime, Josh and I stood up and took a good look at our sea creature wearing sunglasses. He snapped a photo of me next to the sand sculpture to send to my mom.

"I'll tell you, Why," Josh said. "If there's another giant crab in the sand sculpture contest, it will be *Knowhere* near as good as yours."

"Please please please say yes," Fiona begged me a few days later. "At least try it once."

"Snorkeling sounds like fun," I said. What I thought was, *for other people!* "But not today, sorry."

"You love trying new things," Fiona pouted, with a hurt look on her face. "You even said yourself that there's not much for you to do at the Shack. We've had two cancellations on the snorkeling tours and both times you've had an excuse why you can't come out with us. Tell me the real reason."

I groaned. "OK, here's the deal. I'm afraid of swimming with real, live fish!"

Fiona was quiet as she thought about it for a minute.

She must think I'm a scaredy-cat, I worried.

"You know, I'm afraid of something, too," she told me, and then added, "actually a few things."

I couldn't believe it. My stepsister seemed so sure of herself. "You are?"

Fiona nodded. "Remember that weekend that Mom and Dad got married? Being in the city with all those cars and the noise made me feel totally out of place. I got dizzy and queasy being on the 26th floor of that skyscraper. To tell you the truth, I'm afraid of heights."

"But you live in the top of a tree!" I said.

That made us both laugh.

"After that trip," Fiona continued, "I promised myself that when we take you to the city at the end of the summer, I'm going to go back up into that skyscraper. And you know what I'm going to do? I'm going to march right over to the big windows and look down. I'm going to face my fear."

"I'll go with you," I told her.

Fiona is brave, I thought. *Can I possibly make a promise to myself to get up my nerve and go in the ocean again?*

Chapter Eight

A BUSINESS IS BORN

That night, the moon was glowing bright and big in the starry sky. It seemed like I could almost reach out and touch it from my hammock by the window. A fresh ocean breeze swept through the room.

Pop had just turned off the solar lantern. Iris, Fiona and I were already tucked in.

My dad stretched out in his hammock, which made small squeaks until it stopped swinging.

"You know," he said, "a lot of customers at the Surf Shack have been asking if we sell snacks."

"Do you want us to pick up granola bars or banana chips when we take the ferry to the mainland tomorrow?" Iris asked.

"Well, I get the feeling that people want something healthy but more filling," he replied.

We were all mulling* that over. The only noises came from the animals and insects in the forest and the waves on the beach.

Finally Pop made a suggestion. "You know that old blender on the counter?"

"You think people would like to munch on our flowers?" Fiona joked.

"No," Pop said with a laugh. "Coral said she wanted to 'do' something this summer. How about using the blender to make smoothies?"

"Flower smoothies?" I asked jokingly.

"Yuck!" Fiona said.

"You girls are silly," he teased. "I was thinking about fruit smoothies. Sort of like a couple of years ago when you had a lemonade stand, Coral. Do you remember?"

"Oh, yeah! That was so much fun!" I exclaimed.

"Great idea!" Fiona chimed in.

We made plans from our hammocks under the light of the moon that shined through the window.

"You could clear out the storage hut next to the Surf Shack and use it for the stand," Iris said. "We could ask Josh's mom, Jane Dilly, if she would sell some of her fruit to you."

"That would be great for everybody," my dad agreed. "The stand would get the most delicious pineapples, bananas and kiwi on the island, and Jane Dilly would get more business."

"There's one huge problem," I told them.

"What?" they all asked at once.

"There's no electricity to run the blender," I told them.

"Oh, that," Pop said. "Grump works miracles when it comes to bicycles. I bet he can even figure out a way to use a bike to power that blender."

A boat powered by the sun and now a blender powered by a bike, I thought. *Who knew?!*

"I'll call it the Bike-and-Blend Smoothie Hut!" I hooted.

I was so excited about running my own business. While everyone else was sleeping, I dreamed up smoothie recipes with fun names with a city theme, like Snazzy Skyscraper Strawberry Smoothie, Beep-Beep! Banana Kiwi Cooler and City Citrus Shake.

The next morning, instead of walking to the Surf Shack, we drove in Pop's white SUV. We had gotten up extra early to pack the blender and a cutting board, and buy ice, straws, napkins and paper cups at the market.

While I cleared all the junk out of the storage hut, cleaned the place up, put out a recycling bin, and wrote the menu on the old chalkboard, Grump was hooking the blender up to a pink bike with streamers on the handlebars and a white basket on the front.

Every once in a while he hooted nonsense* like "Marflee-jiggin-snaff!" and "Rotten rifflenickly already!"

I had no idea what it meant, but it did not sound like things were going well. I wondered if

the bike-and-blend idea would really work.

My dad told Jane Dilly about our plan. Within an hour, the Pineapple Princess and Josh showed up with a cart full of fruit.

"What do you think?" I asked them proudly.

I fanned my arms open to show them the new and improved hut.

"It's just what this beach needs," Jane Dilly stated.

"Biggie huffa-huffa humdinger!" Grump said as he set the bike right in front of the Smoothie Hut. The blender was screwed onto a board over the back fender of the bike.

Grump checked out the menu on our sign. "I'll take one Snazzy Skyscraper Strawberry Smoothie, please."

I wasn't sure how to turn the blender on.

"Just add the fruit to the blender, put the lid on and start pedaling," Grump ordered. "When the back wheel spins, the blades inside the blender begin turning."

"Why is the back wheel on a stand?" I asked.

"So the wheel doesn't touch the ground," Grump replied. "That way the bike will stay in one place and not move forward."

My dad was right. Grump does work miracles.

From the expression on Grump's face, the first smoothie I made was tasty.

"It's like sipping ice cream through a straw," he said.

"Thank you, Grump," I said. "Normally, customers will pay for smoothies at the Surf Shack, but for all your hard work today, the smoothie is free."

People on the beach were interested in why there was a blender on a bike. They would come over to find out what it was all about, and then end up buying a creamy, ice-cold smoothie.

Josh helped out at the Bike-and-Blend

Smoothie Hut sometimes, too. I'd take orders from the customers while he took a turn cycling.

As he huffed and puffed, pedaling faster and faster, he'd joke, "I'm going *Knowhere*—fast!"

We chatted while we worked. Josh told me how his school tennis team is on a winning streak* (nine tournaments in a row) and how lucky Fiona and I are to be glamping.

Glamping…not that word again! I thought. Just as I was about to ask what it meant, three customers got in line for smoothies.

We had only been open for a couple of days and business was already booming*.

Chapter Nine

FLIBBERBUMBLES

Yahoo! I'd never felt a rush of excitement like this before. What a thrill to be up on the surfboard, riding a wave!

This is fantastic! I thought.

What had I ever been so scared of? A crab that was really an empty shell? A piece of seaweed that's not much different than grass? It was no big deal.

As the power of the wave carried me in to the shore, I felt perfectly happy.

Surfing is what I want to do for the rest of my summer! I thought.

A strong breeze nearly knocked me over. I shook it off, not wanting to lose my balance on the surfboard. Then the breeze grabbed my arm. *Wait a minute, a breeze can't do that,* I thought.

"Why!" Fiona whispered, lightly touching my arm. "Wake up. We overslept. You're going to be late opening the Smoothie Hut."

I jolted* up in my hammock. A dream. The thrilling wave ride had only been a dream.

ॐ ॐ

I couldn't get the dream out of my mind the whole day while I was at the Bike-and-Blend Smoothie Hut. It had seemed so real. And had felt so exciting.

I knew what I wanted to do. After the hut closed that afternoon, I quickly changed into my wetsuit and grabbed my surfboard.

Josh and Fiona were just about to run out into the waves when they saw me.

"Seriously, Why?" Josh said. "You're actually going to surf with us?"

"Yessssss!" Fiona cried as she gave me a high five.

My dad looked at me in surprise. "Alright!"

Pop went over the surfing basics with me

again. "I think you're ready, Coral."

"I'm ready," I agreed. "Let's go!"

I was wobbly on the surfboard and wiped out a bajillion times.

It didn't matter that I couldn't quite get the hang of it yet. Just getting out there in the waves was a huge accomplishment for me.

Business at the Smoothie Hut was so good over the next week that I hardly had time to

practice making my sand sculptures.

As it turned out, Grump was one of our best smoothie customers.

Lots of expert surfers came to the Smoothie Hut. When Fiona was helping out, some of them signed her autograph book, which she kept in the basket on the front of the bike.

Josh, Fiona and I had a good system going. One person would pedal, one person would take orders, put the fruit into the blender and pour it into cups, and one person would clean the blender in between making smoothies.

We were going through so many crates of pineapples, bananas and kiwi that Jane Dilly had to deliver fruit twice a day.

Then out of the blue, while we were making a City Citrus Shake, the whirring* noise of the old blender turned from R–R–r–r–r–r- to no sound at all.

No matter how fast or slow we pedaled the bike, the blade inside the blender wouldn't turn.

Grump came to our rescue. Using a

screwdriver, he unscrewed the blender from the back of the bike and brought it into his work area in the Surf Shack. Soon all the tiny pieces from inside the blender were scattered across the workbench.

"What's wrong with it? Why did it stop?" I asked Grump.

"Skit-scat!" Grump growled, swatting us away.

As we watched Grump "perform surgery" on the poor old blender, I saw Fiona's face pinch up and her eyebrows form a frown.

"I'm sorry, Fiona," I told her. "I know you were really happy that we were a blender family."

Fiona looked at me strangely. Then a smile crept across her face and she began giggling uncontrollably. "A *blended* family, not a *blender* family!"

"What?" I asked. "What is a blended family?"

Fiona explained: "A blended family is one with two parents who each have their own kids and they come together to form a new family. That's us—two families *blended* together—you and your dad, and me and my mom. And now we're sisters forever."

I liked that idea. A lot.

While we waited to hear if the blender could be saved, Fiona and I passed the time by playing Mancala in the sand.

While we played, we heard, "Awww fiddlesticks!" "Fer the love of popcorn!" and "FLIBBERBUMBLES!" coming from the Surf Shack.

If Grump the miracle worker is frustrated, I thought, *we are in big trouble.*

Oh, dear. It certainly looked like the Bike-and-Blend Smoothie Hut was going out of business as quickly as it had started.

Chapter Ten

FACING MY FEARS

Fiona sat on the bike and I slumped against the counter of the Smoothie Hut.

Grump appeared before us, wiping the sweat off his forehead with the back of his hand. "Phew! I need a smoothie," he announced. "A Beep-Beep! Banana Kiwi Cooler sure would taste good right now."

Fiona and I shot each other confused glances. Then we saw something we'd never seen before.

Grump smiled. Maybe for the first time ever.

He chuckled to himself and trotted back to the Surf Shack. When he returned, he screwed the blender onto the bike.

"You're back in business," he told us. "And I've worked up a thirst for one of those scrump-dilli-iscious smoothies of yours!"

Fiona scrambled over to the cooler and grabbed the ingredients. I jumped onto the bike and started pedaling.

The blender loudly whirred and hummed.

"Hooray!" Fiona and I shouted.

We knew the way to Grump's heart. As a thank you, we promised Grump free smoothies for life.

"Jackpot-yippie-yay-yay zibberdyzash!" he whooped happily.

Later that afternoon, Fiona, Josh and I presented Grump with an unusual gift. We didn't have a gift box, so we'd hollowed out a pineapple and put the present inside.

He scrunched up his face. "What's this?"

"It's a little thank you," Fiona said.

"From the three of us," Josh added.

"For me?!" Grump asked.

"Open it!" we all cheered.

Grump lifted the lid of green leaves off the top of the pineapple. He peered* inside and pulled out a nametag we'd made for him.

> **Welcome to the Surf Shack! My name is**
> # Mr. Fix-it

He pinned it below his Grump nametag and tapped his forehead with his finger. "I like the clever nametag and the fancy container it came in."

Pop gave me surfing lessons whenever business slowed down at the Surf Shack. A couple of champion surfers who were visiting the island also took the time to give me some pointers.

Even though I started out as a total flop* at surfing, I kept practicing. The better I got, the more confidence I had.

My eyes were always darting around the water, checking for imaginary giant child-eating crabs and sharks. Since I didn't see anything but clear, clean water, pebbles and seashells, I was able to put my fear in the back of my mind and relax.

One day, I finally stood up on the surfboard and rode a wave!

What a feeling! This time it was for real, not just a dream!

Josh ran up to me when I got to the beach. "Why! Congratulations! Do you *Knowhere* there's a lot of pride for you? Right here!"

He spread his arms wide to show my dad, Iris, Fiona and all the people on the beach cheering for me.

"Way to go, Coral!" "Yahooooo, Why!" "You did it!"

I knew my mom was going to be so proud of me, too.

Me. City-girl Coral. Surfing in the ocean!

I'd faced my fear and was ready to take on the world. As Grump might say, "Wowie-zowie WOOT-WOOT!"

Before long, I was hooked on surfing and wanted to know anything and everything about surfboards. I probably drove Grump bonkers

asking a million questions.

"What's longboarding? How is it different from shortboarding?" I asked.

He explained that longboarding is best for long, gentle waves and, like the name says, it's done with a longer surfboard.

Shortboarding uses shorter boards that are easier to handle for doing quick turns and performing tricks.

"What causes a rip current*?" I asked. "What is hang ten*?" "What's a goofy* foot?"

"Thank goodness," Grump grumbled when a customer showed up and he could escape from my questions.

The competition was a few days away and the island was buzzing* with excitement.

It was time to "shake" things up at the Bike-and-Blend Smoothie Hut with a new menu. Fiona, Josh and I wrote the flavors on the chalkboard.

Menu

Go Coconuts Super Cycler
Thirsty Surfer's Delight
Island Mango Magic
Beachside Breeze Punch
Take-a-Break Banana Shake

"Mmmmmm, I can't wait to try the new flavors," my dad said. "But first, I want to give you the money that the Smoothie Hut has earned so far."

Since our customers paid for their smoothies at the Surf Shack, I hadn't even thought about the money. By the look of surprise on Josh and Fiona's faces, they hadn't either.

Pop set a medium-sized, heavy box on the counter. "You can decide how to split the cash or what to do with it. And by the way, after we subtracted the money to pay for the fruit and other ingredients, you have quite a lot of profits* leftover. Good job!"

"I just helped out when I could," Fiona said.

"You take the money, Coral."

Josh agreed.

"I couldn't have done it without you both," I told them. "Working together is what makes it fun. I think we should all decide what to do with the money."

We came up with lots of ideas, but one stood out. Since the money came from customers who are surfers or who appreciate surfing, maybe it should go toward the sport.

"I bet other kids in the city—kids like me—would love to learn how to surf, too," I said.

"What if we used the profits at the Bike-and-Blend Smoothie Hut to help kids take surfing lessons?" Josh suggested.

"Maybe for one week during the summer," Fiona added, "the ferryboat could bring kids from the mainland out to Knowhere during the day and bring them back in the late afternoon?"

"Great idea!" I agreed. "We could call it the City Surfers Summer Camp."

Pop was really excited about starting a camp. He invited a few people to a campfire dinner meeting to see if we could make it happen the following year.

As we all sat by the campfire, we cooked our food and tossed ideas around.

Iris volunteered to ferry the kids back and forth on The Triple Dip.

Pop said he would pick kids up from the ferry in the SUV and bring them to the beach. He would also be in charge of teaching kids how to surf.

Two young surfers, Jess and Chris, who are both on their way to being pros, said they would volunteer for the week to help teach, too.

Grump offered to take the campers on a bike tour of the island using the Shack's rental bikes.

Josh's dad Andy, who is a lawyer, promised to look into any legal rules and permits* for running a camp.

"The Surf Shack doesn't have enough surfboards for all the campers," Pop worried, "so

we'll have to buy more, and they're not cheap."

"With the surfing competition coming up, there will be lots of thirsty customers," I said. "I think we'll be able to raise the money."

"I'll sell my fruit to the Smoothie Hut for what I buy it for," Jane Dilly said, "so that will save money."

"Sounds like we'll be hosting the first City Surfers Summer Camp next year!" I said.

"Dillydally-flingflang!" Grump exclaimed as we all laughed. "Now let's eat! I vote that we start with the sunbaked apple pie that Fiona made."

❧ ❧

The next day, Josh and I were working on my latest sand sculpture, a ladybug sitting on a leaf, when Fiona came running up to the Smoothie Hut. She was out of breath and her cheeks were pink.

"Come on!" she said excitedly. "There were two last-minute cancellations for the snorkeling tour this afternoon! You can both come!"

Oh, my! I thought. *I'm just not sure. Surfing is one thing. You're not right in the water swimming with fish.*

"I really can't close the Smoothie Hut," I said. "It starts to get busy in about an hour."

"I've got that covered," she said. "Jane Dilly will run it while you and Josh are on The Triple Dip."

"But..." I said.

Fiona took me by the hand. "No buts. You're a surfer and pretty soon you'll be a snorkeler."

"OK," I said, but I was not at all sure it was.

We motored out in the Triple Dip to a spot that was perfect for snorkeling.

Dangling my legs over the back of the boat, I took a deep breath. It took all the courage I had to get my life vest, fins and mask on, put the snorkel into my mouth, and slip into the water.

Iris and Fiona were floating just a few feet away.

At first, everything seemed just fine. *I can do this,* I thought. Then all of a sudden, a huge school of fish (and I'm talking hundreds of fish!) began swimming right at me. EEEEEEEK!

Chapter Eleven

GLAD TO BE GLAMPING

I felt like I couldn't breathe. My heart was pounding. I was kicking my swim fins wildly to get to the side of the boat. *Get a grip on yourself!* I thought.

Then, as fast as the fish had come toward me, they were gone.

Phew! That wasn't so bad, I thought. *In fact, it was pretty amazing.*

Another larger fish with gorgeous blue and yellow stripes came near me. I tried to calm myself. I looked at him and he noticed me. When I fluttered my fins, off he went.

Why, he's as scared of me as I am of him, I thought.

As I became more comfortable, I noticed silvery fish in all shapes and sizes, decorated in

every color of the rainbow. Below me was a forest of sea plants and coral swaying in the clear water. The underwater world was fascinating.

I'd gotten to know a whole kingdom of creatures that lives in the treetops and a whole kingdom that lives on the floor of the ocean.

The following day, two teenage sisters stopped by the Smoothie Hut, but they weren't there to order.

"Do you have a vending machine here? I want a soda," whined the sister wearing the pink bikini.

"No, we don't," I said. "There are no vending machines on the island. But there is a market in the village."

"So you don't have any vending machines, movie theaters or coffee shops here...what's up with this island?" huffed the sister wearing a yellow beach cover-up dress.

"What's *up* on this island," Fiona proudly

told the girls, "is the house we live in."

"Do you live on a mountain or something?" the girls asked.

"No, we're glamping," Fiona replied. "In a tree house."

Oh, no, I thought, *Fiona and her riddles.*

"I think I read about that glamping thing," sniffed the girl in the pink bikini.

"You probably did. It's getting popular around the world," Fiona said. "The name glamping is short for glamorous camping. It's for people who like the outdoors, but want to be more comfortable than sleeping in a tent."

So that's what that odd word means! I thought.

The girls were interested. "Can we see your tree house?"

"Let me ask our mom and dad, but I'm sure they'll say yes," Fiona told the girls. "It's pretty great."

"It even has a tunnel slide," I added.

Meeting the girls reminded me about how I'd

reacted when I came to the island.

At first, Knowhere wasn't what I'd imagined. No beach house, no TV and no electricity. But it turned out to be no problem.

Glamping was a ton of fun. I guess that sometimes the unexpected turns out to be better than expected.

The beach was crazy busy the day of the Surfing and Sand Sculpture Competition. Some of the best surfers were there, as well as surfing fans and a television crew that was filming the event.

The three Smoothie Hut managers—Fiona, Josh and me—were all ready to pedal and blend.

Jane Dilly had supplied us with crates and crates of fruit.

"Let's make sure we're all stocked up before the rush begins," I suggested.

"OK," Josh said. "Do we have vanilla?"

"Lots," Fiona stated, as she checked the shelves below the counter.

"Straws?" I asked.

"Plenty," Fiona replied.

"Cups?" Josh asked.

"Ummm, hmmm…" Fiona said. "I can only find about 10 or so."

"Did you look in the box in the corner?" Josh asked.

"Yep," Fiona said. "None in there, either."

I froze*. I hadn't realized that we'd used most

of the cups Iris had brought from the mainland.

"Maybe the little market in the village has some," Josh suggested. "I'll ride my bike over there and find out."

In a flash, he buckled his helmet and rode off.

Five minutes later, he was back, holding one package of 12 cups. "This is all they had."

"Oh, no!" I cried, panicking*. "These won't last more than a half hour today."

"Without cups, how are we going to serve smoothies?" Fiona added sadly.

I knew what all three of us were thinking: *No smoothies means no money for the City Surfers Summer Camp.*

Chapter Twelve

USE YOUR HEAD

I searched around for my dad, and spotted him helping out a customer. *Well, I'm sure Mr. Fix-it will know what to do*, I thought.

I ran over to the Surf Shack and found Grump. He was putting a chain on a purple tandem bike, which two people can ride at once.

"Grump, we need your help!" I begged. "We have an emergency on our hands."

I explained the situation. "We need one of your miracles!"

"You don't need a miracle," he said, tapping his forehead. "You need to use your head."

"Huh?" I said with disappointment.

"You don't even need cups," he continued. "Everything you need is at the Smoothie Hut. Now skedaddle-raddle think-aroo!"

Grump turned his back to me and continued working on the tandem bike.

I told Fiona and Josh what Grump had said. They were as puzzled as I was. We had just three cups left. When those were gone, we'd have to close the stand.

I glanced at all the baskets of bananas and kiwi. *And what are we going to do with the 18 crates of pineapples?!* I wondered.

I thought about something Grump had told us a few days before. He'd called the pineapple gift box a "fancy container." We had 18 crates of fancy containers!

"Let's start scooping the fruit out of the pineapples," I said to Josh and Fiona. "We can use the empty pineapple shells as the cups...."

Fiona knew just what I was talking about. "And use the fruit in the smoothies!"

"That's brilliant!" added Josh. "My mom has a tool called a pineapple corer. It screws into the middle of the pineapple and takes all the fruit out in a few seconds."

"The Pineapple Princess is at your service," Jane Dilly said, holding up her pineapple corer as she peeked around the corner. "I saw the line forming at the Smoothie Hut and thought I'd help out."

There was a line of customers at the Hut all day long. Fiona, Josh and I took turns pedaling, pouring the smoothies, washing the blender and taking orders. We sold every single one of the pineapples.

When the profits from all our sales were counted, we had enough to buy five new surfboards for the campers.

Jane Dilly enjoyed herself so much that day that she offered to take over the Bike-and-Blend Smoothie Hut at the end of the summer. From there she would be able to sell her freshly sliced fruit and make smoothies, too. And she'd continue to set aside the smoothie profits for the City Surfers Summer Camp.

"Where else could I run a business, get exercise by cycling and help kids all at the same time?" the Pineapple Princess asked.

From our spot at the Hut, we also saw most of the surfing competition. The speed and maneuvers of the surfers were beyond exciting!

Although I didn't win in the kids' sand sculpture contest, I did get a ribbon for the Cutest Crustacean*.

The adults' sand sculpture competition was spectacular. The artists each got 12 tons of sand to work with, but they had just 30 hours to complete their sculptures.

Most of the sculptures were so big that they were much taller than I am. There was a three-layer birthday cake complete with a candle, a spaceship and a monkey eating a banana.

⚜

Later that afternoon, Fiona, Josh and I decided to cool off and relax. We waded out into the ocean, sat on my surfboard and talked about the talented surfers and sand artists we'd seen that day.

"Can you believe that the sand artists came from all around the world?" Fiona asked. "Singapore, Canada, Africa, Spain…."

"Imagine how exciting it would be to travel to other countries during summer vacation," Josh said. "I'm not sure where I'd go first."

"Me neither," Fiona told us. "How about you, Coral? If you could go anywhere in the world next summer, where would you go?"

"That's easy," I replied with a smile. "There's nowhere I'd rather be than Knowhere."

Glossary

*Many words have more than one meaning. Here are the definitions of words marked with this symbol ** *(an asterisk) as they are used in this story.*

booming: *growing, being successful*
bow: *the front part of a boat*
buzzing: *being full of activity*
cake, as in "piece of cake": *something that is done easily*
competition: *a contest or challenge*
current, as in "rip current": *water that flows strongly from the shore*
crustacean: *an animal, such as a crab or lobster, that has a hard outer shell*
day, as in "back in the day": *an earlier time in a person's life*
disaster: *an event that causes much damage*
flop: *failure*
froze: *suddenly became still*
glanced: *looked quickly*
glumly: *sadly*
goofy, as in "goofy foot": *putting the right foot forward while surfing*

hilarious: *very funny*

honeymoon: *a vacation people take after they get married*

impatiently: *in an irritated way, not able to wait*

jolted: *moved suddenly*

mainland: *the main part of a country, which is separate from islands nearby*

maneuvers: *movements that require practice and skill*

model: *a small object that is made to look like a larger object*

muffled: *quiet, hard to hear*

mulling: *thinking*

mutter: *speak in a low voice or grumble*

nonsense: *foolish or silly talk*

panicking: *feeling full of fear*

peered: *looked closely*

permits: *official papers that give permission to do something*

preserve: *protect from damage and harm*

profits: *the amount of money left after subtracting the amount it cost to make something*

queasy: *feeling uncomfortable and sick in the stomach*

resources: *useful and valuable things such as clean water and land*

sculpture: *a work of art that has a shape of some kind*

shrugged: *raised shoulders slightly*

snorkeling: *swimming on the surface of the water, using a face mask for underwater viewing and a short breathing tube (snorkel)*

streak, as in "winning streak": *a period of time when success happens*

surf: *waves of the ocean breaking on the shore*

SUV: *abbreviation for "sport-utility vehicle," a type of vehicle that can be driven on paved or unpaved roads*

ten, as in "hang ten": *curling all ten toes over the nose (pointed end) of the surfboard while surfing*

thatched: *made of straw or palm leaves*

throw: *a small blanket*

topsy-turvy: *upside down*

tropical, as in "tropical island": *an island in an area of the world known for hot weather*

tweaks: *little changes*

whined: *spoke in a complaining way*

whirring: *long, low sound*

Beach Mancala

Mancala is a popular board game. But hundreds of years ago, it was played much the same way that Coral, Josh and Fiona played it—by digging small holes in the dirt or sand and using pebbles as playing pieces. If it's a rainy or indoors kind of day, you can also arrange small bowls for your playing board. Marbles, seashells, pumpkin seeds or coins all work as playing pieces. Once you know the rules, you can play this fun game wherever you go.

What you'll need:
• Playing board (Dig 14 small "bowls" or holes in the sand so it looks like the picture below. Wet sand works best.)
• 48 playing pieces (pebbles, tiny seashells or marbles)

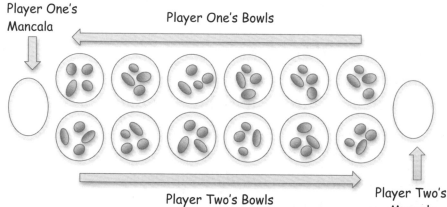

Player One's Mancala

Player One's Bowls

Player Two's Bowls

Player Two's Mancala

To win:

Collect as many pebbles as you can in your Mancala (the storage area at the end of the board) before the other player removes all the pebbles from the six bowls on their side of the board.

How to play:

1. Two players sit on opposite sides of the board. The larger bowl at the end of the board to the right is the player's Mancala. The six bowls in front of each player are their bowls.
2. Place four pebbles in each of the 12 bowls as shown in the drawing.
3. To begin, one player scoops up all of the pebbles in any one bowl on their side of the board.
4. That player then drops one pebble into the bowl to the left of the empty bowl, and continues on around the board to the left by dropping pebbles one at a time in each bowl until the pebbles run out.
5. If you get to your Mancala, drop a pebble into it. If you get to the *other* player's Mancala, skip it and continue dropping pebbles into holes on the other side of the board.
6. If the last pebble in your hand is dropped into *your* Mancala, you get another turn. If not, it's the other player's turn.
7. When all six bowls on one side of the board are empty, the game is over.
8. The player who still has pebbles in any of the six bowls on their side of the board when the game ends adds them to their Mancala.
9. Each player counts the pebbles in their Mancala. The player with the most pebbles is the winner.

The Power of a Girl

For every *Our Generation*® product you buy, a portion of sales goes to Free The Children's Power of a Girl Initiative to help provide girls in developing countries an education—the most powerful tool in the world for escaping poverty.

Did you know that out of the millions of children who aren't in school, 70% of them are girls? In developing communities around the world, many girls can't go to school. Usually it's because there's no school available or because their responsibilities to family (farming, earning an income, walking hours each day for water) prevent it.

Over the past two years, Free The Children has had incredible success with its Year of Water and Year of Education initiatives, providing 100,000 people with clean water for life and building 200 classrooms for overseas communities. This year, they celebrate the Year of Empowerment, focusing on supporting alternative income projects for sustainable development.

The most incredible part is that most of Free The Children's funding comes from kids just like you, holding lemonade stands, bake sales, penny drives, walkathons and more.

Just by buying an *Our Generation* product you have helped change the world, and you are powerful (beyond belief!) to help even more.

If you want to find out more, visit:
www.ogdolls.com/free-the-children

FREE THE CHILDREN
children helping children through education

Free The Children provided the factual information pertaining to their organization.
Free The Children is a 501c3 organization.

this is **our** story

We are an extraordinary generation of girls. And have we got a story to tell.

Our Generation® is unlike any that has come before. We're helping our families learn to recycle, holding bake sales to support charities, and holding penny drives to build homes for orphaned children in Haiti. We're helping our little sisters learn to read and even making sure the new kid at school has a place to sit in the cafeteria.

All that and we still find time to play hopscotch and hockey. To climb trees, do cartwheels all the way down the block and laugh with our friends until milk comes out of our noses. You know, to be kids.

Will we have a big impact on the world? We already have. What's ahead for us? What's ahead for the world? We have no idea. We're too busy grabbing and holding on to the joy that is today.

Yep. This is our time. This is our story.

www.ogdolls.com

this is my favorite family story:

_____

_____

_____

_____

_____

_____

_____

_____

_____

_____

_____

_____

_____

About the Author

Susan Cappadonia Love lives in a purple house in Milton, Massachusetts with her husband, Scott, and daughters, Sophie and Olivia. When she was a kid, one of her favorite places to be was in the tree house that her dad built in her backyard. She has written twelve books in the Our Generation® Series, as well as other children's books.

About the Illustrator

Trish Rouelle has been drawing since she was first able to hold a crayon. Back then it was mostly horses or funny pictures of her brothers. Now she lives in northern Vermont where she draws, paints and photographs the beautiful landscape that she sees when she is out on her mountain bike or hiking with her husband, Jeff, and their daughter, Ella.

This story came to life because of all the wonderful people who contributed their creativity and vision, including Joe Battat, Dany Battat, Karen Erlichman, Loredana Ramacieri, Sandy Jacinto, Véronique Casavant, Véronique Chartrand, Jenny Gambino, Natalie Cohen, Karen Woods, Pam Shrimpton and Joanne Burke Casey.